**WELCOME TO
PASSPORT TO READING**
A beginning reader's ticket to a brand-new world!

Every book in this program is designed to build read-along and read-alone skills, level by level, through engaging and enriching stories. As the reader turns each page, he or she will become more confident with new vocabulary, sight words, and comprehension.

These PASSPORT TO READING levels will help you choose the perfect book for every reader.

READING TOGETHER
Read short words in simple sentence structures together to begin a reader's journey.

READING OUT LOUD
Encourage developing readers to sound out words in more complex stories with simple vocabulary.

READING INDEPENDENTLY
Newly independent readers gain confidence reading more complex sentences with higher word counts.

READY TO READ MORE
Readers prepare for chapter books with fewer illustrations and longer paragraphs.

This book features sight words from the educator-supported Dolch Sight Words List. This encourages the reader to recognize commonly used vocabulary words, increasing reading speed and fluency.

For more information, please visit passporttoreadingbooks.com.

Enjoy the journey!

Little, Brown and Company

Hachette Book Group
1290 Avenue of the Americas, New York, NY 10104
Visit us at lb-kids.com
bobthebuilder.com

Little, Brown and Company is a division of Hachette Book Group, Inc.
The Little, Brown name and logo are trademarks of Hachette Book Group, Inc.

The publisher is not responsible for websites (or their content)
that are not owned by the publisher.

First Edition: October 2016

Library of Congress Number: 2016938032

ISBN 978-0-316-27296-4

10   9   8   7   6   5   4   3   2   1

CW

Printed in the United States of America

Passport to Reading titles are leveled by independent reviewers applying the standards
developed by Irene Fountas and Gay Su Pinnell in *Matching Books to Readers: Using
Leveled Books in Guided Reading*, Heinemann, 1999.

Muck on Ice

Adapted by Emily Sollinger
Based on the episode "Muck on Ice"
written by Douglas Wood

LITTLE, BROWN AND COMPANY
New York   Boston

Attention, Bob the Builder fans!
Look for these words
when you read this book.
Can you spot them all?

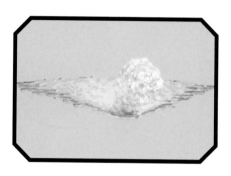

ice

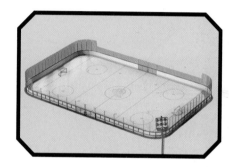

rink

rock

wall

Bob and his team
were building an ice rink.

"Here come the Rockets!" said Leo.
"I cannot wait to see them
play hockey," said Scoop.

"The ice at our rink has melted,"
the Rockets told Bob.
"Can we play our match
here tonight?"

"Our rink is not
ready yet," said Bob.

"Please?" asked the Rockets.

"We can work fast!" said Muck.

Bob agreed.

"Yay!" cheered the Rockets.

"Can we build it?" Bob asked.

"Yes, we can!" said the team.

The team worked hard.
Wendy, Bob, and Two-Tonne
went to get more supplies.

"Now, where do we get
the ice from?" asked Muck.
"We will make it!" said Lofty.

"When it is very cold,
water turns to ice," Leo explained.
"Wow!" said Muck.

Muck pushed a rock with his scoop.
The rock slid across the ice.
"Wow!" said Muck.

Muck followed the rock.

Muck rolled onto the ice rink.

Muck slid on the ice.

Muck went fast.

He hit the rock with his scoop.

"Ice hockey!" said Muck.

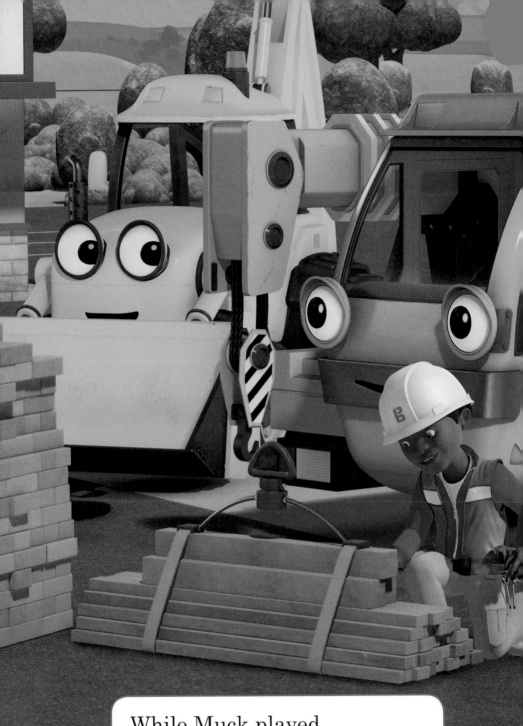

While Muck played,
Leo, Lofty, and Scoop worked.

"Where is Muck?" asked Leo.

"Whee!" shouted Muck.

Muck slid a rock to Scoop.

Scoop slid onto the ice.

Lofty wanted to play.

He slid onto the ice.

"I cannot slow down!"

cried Lofty.

Bob, Wendy, and Two-Tonne
returned with the supplies.
They heard a big crash!

"Uh-oh!" said Bob.

"Watch out!" called Scoop.

Scoop bumped into Muck.

Muck bumped into Lofty.

Lofty bumped into the wall.

The wall fell down.
"How will we fix this
by tonight?" asked Wendy.

Muck had an idea.
"Everything moves faster
on ice," said Muck.

They all worked together.

Muck slid a panel to Scoop.

Bob hammered the posts.

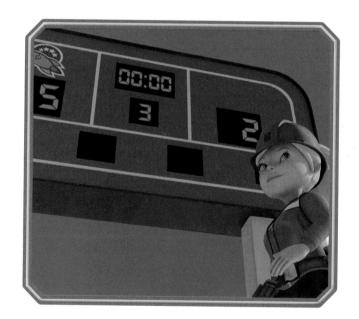

Wendy fixed the scoreboard.

Bob and his team finished
the job just in time.

The Rockets came back.

They were ready to play.

"Thank you!" said the Rockets.

"You are welcome," said Bob.

"Have a great game!"